2025 First US edition
Translation copyright © 2025 by Charlesbridge
Illustrations copyright © 2022 by Joan Turu
All rights reserved, including the right of reproduction in whole or in part
in any form. Charlesbridge and colophon are registered trademarks of
Charlesbridge Publishing, Inc.

At the time of publication, all URLs printed in this book were accurate
and active. Charlesbridge, the author, and the illustrator are not responsible for
the content or accessibility of any website.

Published by Charlesbridge
9 Galen Street, Watertown, MA 02472 • (617) 926-0329 • www.charlesbridge.com

Original title: *¡Mi papá más!*
Text © Fran Pintadera, 2022
Illustrations © Joan Turu, 2022
Originally published by Carambuco Ediciones in Barcelona, Spain.
Rights arranged by IMC Agencia Literaria, SL. All rights reserved.

Illustrations in this US work supported by Institut Ramon Llull.

Library of Congress Cataloging-in-Publication Data
Names: Pintadera, Fran, 1982– author. | Turu, Joan, 1984– illustrator.
Title: My dad is the best / Fran Pintadera; illustrated by Joan Turu.
Other titles: ¡Mi papá más! English
Description: First US edition. | Watertown, MA: Charlesbridge, 2024. |
Originally published by Carambuco Ediciones in Barcelona, Spain. |
Audience: Ages 4–8. | Audience: Grades K–1. |
Summary: "Two boys argue about whose dad is the best and strongest,
taking the competition to the extreme."—Provided by publisher.
Identifiers: LCCN 2023056522 (print) | LCCN 2023056523 (ebook) |
ISBN 9781623544911 (hardcover) | ISBN 9781632894311 (ebook)
Subjects: LCSH: Fathers—Juvenile fiction. | Competition (Psychology)—Juvenile
fiction. | CYAC: Fathers—Fiction. | Competition (Psychology)—Fiction.
Classification: LCC PZ7.1.P5674 Myd 2024 (print) | LCC PZ7.1.P5674 (ebook) |
DDC [E]—dc23
LC record available at https://lccn.loc.gov/2023056522
LC ebook record available at https://lccn.loc.gov/2023056523

Printed in China
(hc) 10 9 8 7 6 5 4 3 2 1

Display type set in Supernet by George Herold-Wildfellner
Text type set in Hank by Bitstream Inc.
Printed by 1010 Printing International Limited in Huizhou, Guangdong, China
Production supervision by Nicole Turner
Designed by Cathleen Schaad

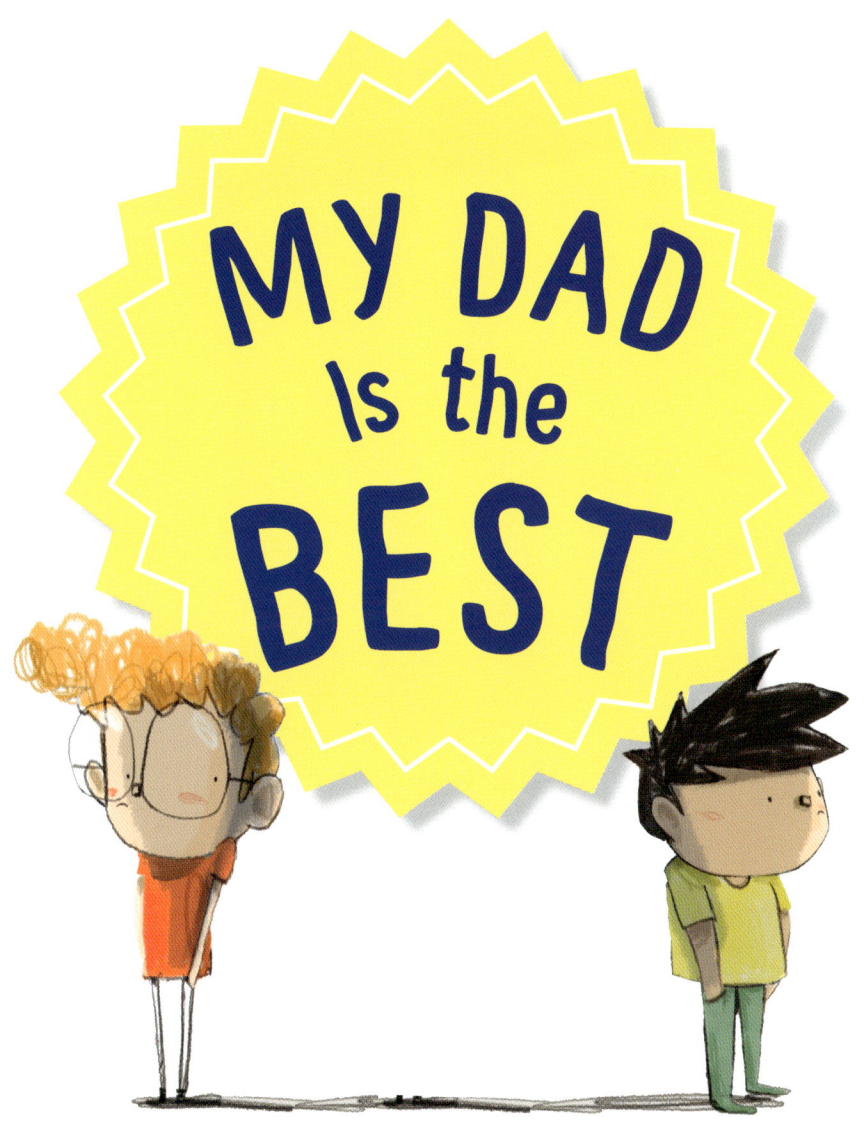

MY DAD Is the BEST

Fran Pintadera

Illustrated by Joan Turu

Charlesbridge

My dad is the best.

My dad is better!

Not possible!
My dad can pick up . . . a truck!

My dad is stronger!
He can pick up a truck . . .

. . . filled with elephants!

Oh, yeah? Well, my dad can pick up
a truck filled with elephants . . .

. . . that are pregnant!

My dad is even stronger!
He can pick up a truck filled with elephants
that are pregnant . . .

. . . with triplets!

Whatever! My dad can pick up a truck filled with elephants pregnant with triplets . . .

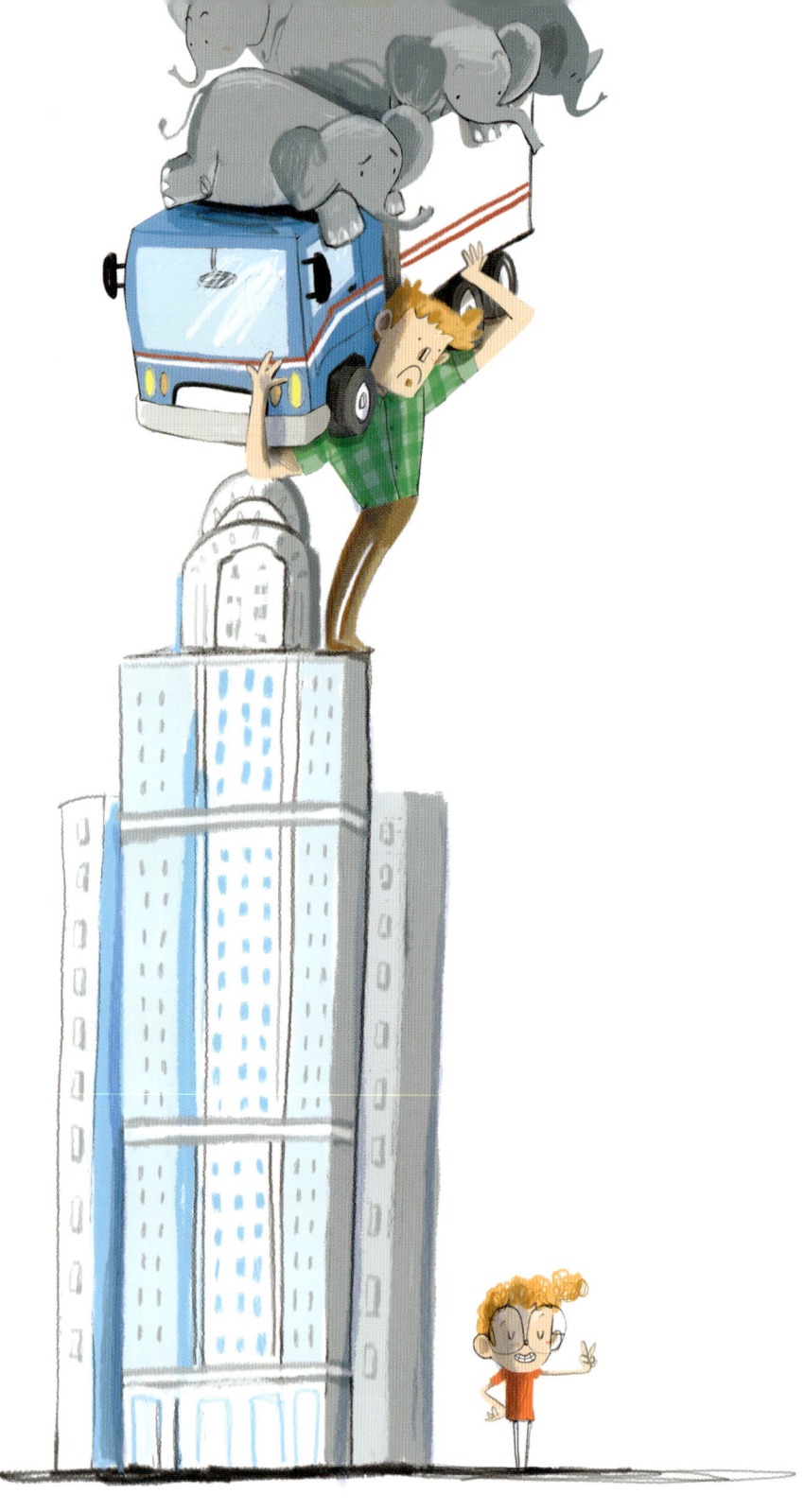

. . . on top of a skyscraper!

My dad is stronger than that!
He can pick up a truck filled with elephants pregnant with triplets on top of a skyscraper . . .

. . . built on a mountain!

Anyone can do that! My dad can pick up
a truck filled with elephants pregnant with triplets
on top of a skyscraper built on a mountain . . .

. . . with one hand!

Well . . .

It seems to me . . .

. . . that my dad . . .

. . . loves your dad.

Well, my dad . . .

. . . loves your dad, too!